A
Little Book
of faery Tales

Written by
Athey Thompson

A Little Book of faery Tales
© Athey Thompson
All Rights reserved

No part of this Book may be reproduced or used in any manner without the express permission of the publisher

ISBN = 978-1-7397800-1-2.

publisher. Athey Thompson
for Sales information please Contact
email. AtheyThompson@yahoo.com

Printed by. promisingprint Ltd
unit 51, Landywood Enterprise park
Hollylane, great Wyrley, Staffordshire.
Tel- 01543 577200

This edition printed in 2022, England

Contents

- 4 ~ Today I shall lose myself
- 5-6 ~ The faeryfolks lucky golden coin
- 7-8 ~ Tale of ye mayday forest faery folk
- 9-10 ~ Tale of the little laughing Elves
- 11-13 ~ Tale of the faerystray
- 14 ~ Oh let me tell thee
- 15-17 ~ The tale of the wee farmer who met ye faeryfolk
- 18 ~ Tale of ye wee tree spirit
- 19-21 ~ Tale of ye hidden faery gate
- 22 ~ Ye old urchin
- 23-24 ~ Tale of ye witch in a bottle
- 25-28 ~ Tale of ye one eyed weasel and ye old hag
- 29 ~ A foolish faery man
- 30 ~ The faery tree
- 31-34 ~ Tale of ye grumpy ogre at the old stone stile
- 35 ~ The mossfolk
- 36 ~ lost in ye old woods
- 37 ~ O'er there
- 38 ~ When they do come
- 39 ~ Tale about the wise old frog
- 40 ~ Thankyou

"Today
I shall lose myself
if only, for a day
A faerytale it shall be"

The faeryfolks Lucky golden Coin

Twas upon a fair midsummers day that I took upon a walk through the old forest. mind, I was half way past the day and wanting to turn back.

When I came upon a wee merry man.
Why dressed in green tweeds And With a Rosy Red cheeks, he Appeared from nowhere. As he stood afoot with a warm smile upon his face.

he did call O'er to me
for he had a message, So I listened Eagerly.

"Why did you know, If ye walk upon a lonely Path And come across a golden Coin.

I Say A golden Coin, Laid down on the ground, Infront of ye, Well ye must pick it up!

for its yours you see

Tis a gift from afar."

Well now, as I wonder I ask the wee man
"Why, Who Would leave me Such a gift."
"Ahh now." he did Say.
Tis the faeryfolk, they Saw you looking
So Sad And they thought, A little good
Luck Ought to Come your Way,
So they have left ye, a golden Coin
    O'er there upon ye ground."

And with that, the wee man was gone
  All but his Words of Wisdom left behind.

Well I never
  Just to think the faeryfolk were Watching
O'er me And they had wished for me
    Such good luck.

Why, their wish alone did fill me
    With Such Joy And made me feel
Much happier than any golden Coin ever Could.

Tale of ye May day forest faery folk

Well now, never did I see such a to do....
I tell thee, that little fella, the one who lives
in a tree in the old forest.

Why, he be such a miserable old fool,
Only the other day he was a shouting and a
bawling at the wee folk.

All they wanted to do was to lay flowers
around the trees, for it was may day eve
ye see.

Well, he did yell out from up in his tree
"What ye little ones want
  Be gone I tell thee
    Be gone,
  Before I fetch me stick."

Why, the Wee faery folk did not hang
About, they ran away as fast as they
Could. With their flowers left behind
Laying on the ground.

Twas on that very night, So I be told
That the faery folk did get their own back.
For the elders had heard all about the
Miserable little fella and his goings on.
And they set to getting Revenge. So they did.

Why, In the dead of night the faeryfolk
They dressed every tree in the old forest
With beautiful flowers and bright Ribbons.
Oh it looked a Mayday dream.
And, As for the Old fella in the tree
Well he never did Say another Word.

Tale of the Little Laughing Elves

Well now, I never did see before my very own eyes. Such a magical sight.

Why, I must tell ye what happened to me. As I took upon a steady stroll, not too far mind. But Into the old forest I did go. Twas such a fine Spring day, with leafy trees And the birds Singing, Oh what a happy day.

Wasn't long, before I reached the old forest glen, Such a peaceful feeling filled the air, As the water trickled gently past, I felt it was a perfect spot for me to rest myself for a while.

So I sat upon a lovely old stone that lay upon the edge of the glen.

Without a care, I sat and pondered Pondered for a while.

Well, Would you believe, from nowhere
    Came the Sound of Laughing....
Why, there be 2 or 3 different Laughs
    Coming from across the glen.
So I Stood up to See, but there was no one
to be Seen, not a Soul to be found.
   And then, the Sound of many tiny foot
Steps Came about from behind me.
    So I Quickly turn around.... And there
Stood Right A front of me Was a group of
Elves, no taller than a foot, Little fellas
All dressed in green tweed And Red Caps.
   With funny little faces And pointed noses
    And bright Red cheeks.
   Why, I just Stood and gawped.
And there they All stood, All around me
    And not a Word was Spoken.
And Within a blink of an eye, they Were gone.
    Just gone.
Well I must tell ye, I did See them, I really did.

Tale of the faery Stray

I'd been a Wandering for days
   Wandering for days, I tell thee
Till I found myself, upon the top
   of an old craggy hill.
I couldn't tell thee how I gotten there
   Not a clue,
Till I remembered meself, Why, it was all
Coming back to me. My foolish Self
for, I had taken a rest upon a faery fort.

Now, there I be, minding my own
As I sat down to rest
   And I thought it be a lovely spot
   to eat my cheese Sandwich.

Oh yes, I'd been looking forward to
eating my cheese sandwich, Twas only
That days freshly baked bread with Butter
And cheese, hmmm it smelt so good..

Ahh, Just as I took my first bite
 A strong wild wind took hold
  from nowhere it came And blew
   Right over me.

Why, It nearly took me flying. Well now,
As I calmed myself. I looked down upon
my lap. And would you believe
  My sandwich was gone!
   gone it was
So I rushed up and looked all over
 But it was nowhere to be seen
  Well I never, I thought
   Where was my Sandwich.

Oh I'd been thinking about my cheese
Sandwich all day, the freshly baked bread
And Thickly Cut cheese.

And In a Moments Rage, I turned and
kicked an old tree trunk, "Take that!
Ye old tree trunk" I did Shout out.

Now then, That be my last memory
Oh Why did I kick that tree trunk.
That be a foolish thing to do.
for that be the faery folks tree trunk
In a faery fort.....
Oh, they must have been So Mad
Dare I Say
They must have Cast a faery stray on me
And A stray I have been until now.

"Oh let me tell thee
How happy I shall be
If every day, I get to be
Sitting here, next to ye"

The Tale of the Wee farmer Who met ye faeryfolk

What fun we did have, As the Sun shined upon a Summers day, And we danced and Singed Songs upon ye meadows.
We made daisychains, We ate Cake and We drinked lots of lovely Tea.
When all of a Sudden

A wee farmer man popped up from behind a tree, And he yelled

"Well now, Well now, all this noise And making Merryment, Tis not cheap, There be a charge! Ooh yes now, Let me See."

Well what an odd wee man he be, dressed In Scraffy green tweeds, Wispy Red hair And matching cheeks.

He stood afront of us as he rubs his chin and has a think....

"Ooh yes, I have it, I Wants A 11 pence, A 12 pence and A 16 pence, That be very nice" he did Say.

"Well now, Why Would We be paying you any Money?" I asked.

"Ahh Well, ye See, you be on me land and I Says So, So I does." he Said.

"The 11 pence be for sitting on my fine grass Would you just look, Tis the finest grass in town And you be Crushing on me daises.

The 12 pence be for all that dancing you be doing on me fine grass

And the 16 pence be, Well it be for all the Singing you be doing, you lot Woke me up With all that merryment, So there That be it."

As soon as the Wee farmer man shut up
A farmer lady came rushing from behind
the tree, Looking mighty Angry.

She whacked the farmer man over the
head with her dusting stick!
"Be gone, Be gone ye old fool
   you be picking on the faery folk,
Youll be ashamed of yourself
   Youll be bringing us bad luck."...
      She yelled.
"Now get home, And no more be said
   from ye, do ye hear me."
She said out loud as she chased him
Back behind the tree. And, We never did
See that funny Wee farmer man again.

17

Tale of ye Wee Tree Spirit

I Wonder, did you See me, See me you did
Why, I'm Sure of that, for I Was a hiding, As I hide
A lot ye See, tis my nature.

'Twas only as you passed on by, Why If
only for a Moment, you did See me as I be hiding
down neath the roots of my old Oak tree. In my
hidey hole I be, happily minding my own.

And you, you were walking upon Such a Sad
Lonesome path, And as you passed on by,
I Saw Such a look of Joy upon your face
Why, the Sparkle in your eyes as you Smiled O'er
at me with Such glee.

Ahh, but I, I did not Smile back, for you See
Tis forbidden to befriend a human child
And for that, I do Regret....
For you Seemed So very lost As you Carried your
heavy heart, Why If only I had Smiled back
And let you know
That I, I did See you too.

Tale of ye hidden faery gate

Oh let me take thee
for a little walk
Into the forest
And far away....

Down upon this old pathway is where we shall go And go shall we, to where the overgrown hedgerows And tall wild flowers do grow. Why, This old pathway has long been forgotten.

And as we do go, furer furer down the path We come upon a Lone hawthorn Tree, full of Blossom Oh so magical it be, All of a sudden a strange feeling takes hold, And it feels like we are no Longer Alone.

Ahh, it is not long now, until we shall Come upon a little wooden gate.

But SShhhh Tis a Secret gate....

Tis a faery gate, And not many folk, Will ever See Such a gate, Ohh but me I have Seen it! Ohh yes I have indeed.

Now let me tell thee, As it was a mystery how I came about it, As I was lost you see. And with the path So overgrown I couldn't See my way home. So I sat for a while And thats when I saw it, There was a little gate.

Why, Id never Seen it before, So I went up to it And knocked upon its knocker.
A knock, A knock, A knock....
And I waited for a while.
But there was no reply.
So I knocked again
A knock, A knock, A knock....
But still there was No reply.

Hmmm.... So I stood peeping through the holes of the wooden gate. And all of a sudden
  A tap, A tap, A tap....
Why, Someone was tapping on my shoulder.
As I turn around, I see a Robin fluttering in the air, Well he looked a little miffed
  As he landed on a branch of a tree.
  "Now then" said the Robin.
"My dear, you must not never, ever knock
  upon a faery gate, Tis not your gate
  to knock upon."
  And with that he flew away.
Well now, I was so a gasp to hear a Robin speak,
  Ohh I tell thee, I soon found my way home.

And since that day, I have looked many a time down that old pathway, for that little wooden gate, But never have I ever seen it again.

  So today, I hope we see it
    I hope we do.

Ye old urchin

Why, he be a sneaky, no good pest of a
faery man. With a feather in his hair he
does come and go. Lurking behind mossy
stones or nestled in tall flower beds.
  Does he wait, oh so silently still
he perches, awaiting to cause mischief.
Why, he bothers not who be his prey.
  For he loves to tease and torment
Any poor folk that come his way.
  Oh a beast he be
    And my advice would be, if ye
        did come across he
    Turn around and count to three
      A one, A two, A three.
And shout out "Be gone will thee"
  And for sure, gone he will be.

Tale of ye Witch in a Bottle

Why, I put that Witch, that Wicked old Whining Witch In a bottle, So I did.

Dare She. To Curseth me, O her Wretched Mind hath turned And She Was Wanting on me to be bad, And bad I shalt not be.

You See, She knew I Was a healer, A good doer Was I, healing the poorest of the poor, T'was not a penny That I asked for. Ah but many a time a gift of Ale I Would agree upon.
And that be the Way I did things.

Oh, but this old Witch, Withered and Waned, She Wanted my Secrets....
Secrets I Shall never Tell.

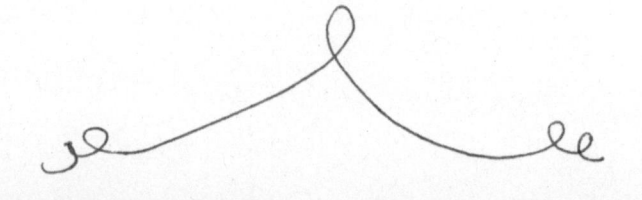

23

Why, I knew she would bring me trouble
So I called upon ye faeryfolk
Who very kindly told me of a spell....

So on that fearful day
That she did come for me
I stood a foot of her And stared into her darkened weary old eyes.

Holding in my hand an empty glass bottle
And a stopper in the other.
I cast out the faery spell
And as soon as I did
She flew into my glass bottle
And
Inside she shall stay.

Tale about ye One eyed Weasel And ye old hag.

There be many a tale told about the old hags And their Comings and goings. Why, they be well known in these parts of County Wicklow. But theres one Curious Tale that I did hear And it goes A bit like this.

Many A year ago there be a young farming family who lived down the way, O'er there. They kept Cows And grew potatoes. The one daughter, she looked after a few chickens, And she thought kindly towards her chickens And they did lay nice big eggs. So one day, When she found a chicken was missing, well she wasn't too happy. Why, that Very day she went searching All over, but her beloved chicken was nowhere To be found.

Whilst out and about she came upon a local farmer who told her, he had seen a one eyed weasel heading towards her farm that very night before.

Ohh she just knew it be that sly old weasel who lived o'er the way. So off she headed to give him a what for.....

Now the weasel with the one eye lived deep within the old forest, where noone ever dared to go. As its known to be the home of ye old hags.

Not being scared at all, off the young girl marches into the old forest. And there she comes right onto the path of an old hag..

"Now child, tell me
 Why have you come so far
  Into ye old forest "

"Why, did noone tell ye
 I say tell ye
of the dangers, for here within the darkened
old forest, 'tis where the lost souls wander.
 They be the foolish ones
  Who crossed the faeryfolk,
Oh, thou shalt not never cross a faery
Oh but they did, And now they live
Between worlds, they be neither Alive no dead
forever they be Cursed, Cast Away, to dwell
within this dark old forest.
 So if I were you, I'd go child
  Before it be too late."
  Said the old hag.

"Well, Im looking for that old weasel, the one
with one eye, hes stolen from me, one of my
chickens, And I want her back."
 Said the young girl.

27

My child, that Weasel has long gone
for I Cast him away, hes forever gone.
Why, that Sneaky no good little Weasel
He thought he could outwit me.
O' how he was wrong
Well good Riddance I do say
And as for your chicken
Well it did get away
May it return to you, or may it not
That's not my Concern
So my child, If you don't move out of my
Sight, Well I Shall Cast ye away too..
Said the old hag.

With that Said, the young girl fled back
home. Now Whether her chicken went
home, I never did know.

A foolish faery man

Oh a foolish faeryman he be
To fall asleep underneath that tree
Why I must tell thee
Thats where I did see
A running wild underneath that tree
Must have been a good thirty three
Little elves, with red caps on they be
Oh mind they be trouble I tell ye
Oh no, I would not never be
Sleeping underneath that tree

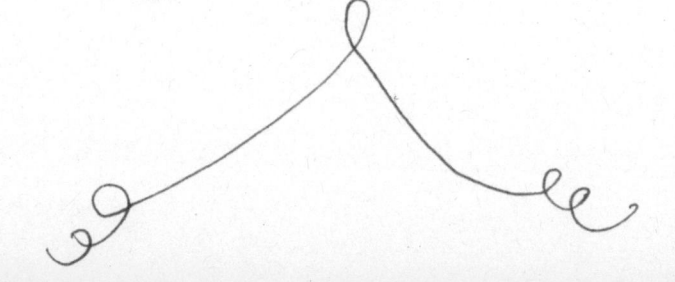

The faery Tree

Well now, never did I ever see such a
magical little tree, with its twisted moss
covered boughs And branches. And as I
   stood afoot of its leafy glare
      I heard a whisper, A whisper it did

   O, Come a little closer
         Closer to me
   O, Come a little Wander
         Wander With me
   O, Come With me
         And ye shall see
   O, Come With me
         See All that Shall be....

Ohh what an enchanted old tree this be
Mind, I shall not share its Secrets for now
   for its Secrets shall be its to share.

Tale of ye grumpy ogre
At the Old stone stile

Well I must hurry on along
If I'm to get home
    But time is not on my side.

You see
   I've been down to the market
    As it be market day, with a long list
I had to fetch.
   But I've been a dawdling, Oh I do that a lot.
And now I'm running late. So I'm rushing
And I'm not thinking straight.

  I take a short cut down the old lanes
    I go, Oh but that was not a great Idea.

For that very short cut
   Takes me over the old stone stile
    And I'd fergot
      About him....

Oh, there he be
    Stood upon the old stone stile
Why, Tis the Ogre stood afoot
    With such a look upon his face
Hes a short fella, with a humped back
A walking stick And a lumpy old face
    He grunts, he groans
        As he sees me coming.

For this stile is no normal stile
    Oh this be his stile....
    And no one shall pass
        Without his say so.
Why, slowly I approach
    Wishing to turn back
        But it's too late
    He does greet me
    "Now then, What will it be
        Shall ye pass
            Or shall ye not."

Why, the choice be yours
    Be it a coin in me hand
      Or be it not....
Oh but be told, Only a coin shall let ye
Pass, So what shall it be."
      He said to me.

Well now, I thinks, a coin I have not got
But what if I could pay another way.
    Why, Ive got a freshly baked meat pie
      So I offers him my pie.

"Meat pie, ye say, Hmmm" he grunts
" Why I likes a meat pie so I does
    Now how about something sweet
      I likes sweet pudding."
      He said to me.

Well Ive an apple pie in my basket
    So I offers him that too.

"Apple pie ye say Mmmm" he grunts.
"Why I likes an apple pie so I does
Now how about a drink?
I likes me a nice drink"
He said to me.
Well, Ive a bottle of stout in my basket,
So I offers it to him.
"Bottle of stout ye say Mmmm" he grunts.
"I likes a bottle of stout I does, So this be
what I shall do, I shall take your meat pie,
Apple pie and bottle of stout, And In return
Ye shall pass through my stile."
He said to me.
Ahh that be a pretty rotten deal if you ask me
But sure enough. I pass over my meat pie,
Apple pie and stout, And soon I'm on my way
Over the old stone stile.
As Im heading home I does think, Well Ive
No meat pie, no Apple pie, And I'm a bottle of
Stout down, Oh there will be trouble
When I does get home.

The Mossfolk

O'er there, far far away we go, deep into the woods is where ye may come upon the Mossfolk. Where ye find Trees with spindly old twisted branches covered in dewy, damp green Moss.

Why these trees be the home to the mossfolk, Some say they be the greenfolk, or ye forestfolk, Or some do say they be the fueryfolk who do dwell within the moss of treetrunks, Logs or Boughs.

The Mossfolk be a Curious Clan of fuery. They hide deep away In the Woods where the damp does settle. These folk be foragers for they Roam around the Woodland with the nature spirits, And the tree spirits, Why, they do live happily Amongst the trees.

So if you ever come upon an old log or fallen Tree Covered In Moss, Well, be mindful of ye Mossfolk And leave them well alone.

Lost in ye old Woods

Well, I know these old Woods well enough
But today I got meself a bit lost, why
I came upon a Crossroads that I'd never
  come upon before. Well, I could go left,
or I could go Right or I could go straight on.
  Feeling muddled, I looked up at the
Tree which was stood in the middle of the
crossroads, And there in the tree, I did see

A wee tree spirit, who did say to me
"When ye're lost, ye're lost
  If ye must, ye must trust
    Ye self will know
      Which way to go."

And with that, he was gone,
  So I took his words of wisdom
  And I wandered on.

O'er there
  Is where we shall go
And go shall we
for hidden away
far, far away
A faery once did say
"Betwixt ye trees
Betwixt ye branches
Betwixt ye leaves
Is where we do meet
Is where we do wait
    Ye See
And if ye shall pass on by
If ye might
Stand neath a tree
  And take a sip
from a dew drop
  On a leaf
Well, ye might just see."
So O'er there
  Is where we shall go
    And go shall we.

When they do come
From neath an earthy mound
They do come
O'er from meadows deep
When they do come
There be no sound
They come
To forage And to feed
And if ye shall
Be kind enough to leave
A share, it shall be known
Of butter, cheese or milk
Left outside upon the ground
And when they do come
At night, just mind, it shall be found
And the passers by
  Who pass by
    Shall bless you
      In return
And leave you
    Well alone.

Tale about the Wise old frog.

'Twas a fine Sunny Summers day down upon the pond where ye old frog did sit upon a large lily pad, happily passing away the day.

When a little voice did come from within the weeping willow tree. for there hidden within the branches crouched a little girl.

And she asked the frog

"Oh, why are you always so happy?"

Well now, the frog, he sat and pondered for a while .... And he answered.

"Why I am happy because I am a frog."

With that, the little girl did come out from beneath the willow branches And stood afoot of the frog.

"Why, thats a funny Answer." Said the girl.

"Well my child it's very simple, lots of folk are unhappy because they want to be someone else. But I my dear, I am happy to be a frog."

I'm over the Moon
That you have purchased
One of my Little Books
Thankyou.

My Little Books Available
A Little Book of Poetry
A Little Book of faery Tales
A Little Book of folk Tales

You may follow me

facebook . Tales of the old forest faeries
Instagram . AThey.Thompson